SPENCE
AND THE MEAN OLD BEAR

Story and Pictures by Christa Chevalier

ALBERT WHITMAN & COMPANY, NILES, ILLINOIS

Also by Christa Chevalier
Little Green Pumpkins
Spence and the Sleepytime Monster
Spence Isn't Spence Anymore
Spence Makes Circles
The Little Bear Who Forgot

Library of Congress Cataloging in Publication Data

Chevalier, Christa.
  Spence and the mean old bear.

  Summary: Angry at his mother, Spence draws a mean old
bear who comes to life to take her away—and then, is
Spence sorry!
  [1. Anger—Fiction. 2. Mothers and sons—Fiction.
3. Bears—Fiction] I. Title.
PZ7.C42557S1 1986   [E]   86-1570
ISBN 0-8075-7572-0

The text of this book is printed in sixteen-point Optima

Text and illustrations © 1986 by Christa Chevalier
Published in 1986 by Albert Whitman & Company, Niles, Illinois
Published simultaneously in Canada by General Publishing, Limited, Toronto
Printed in U.S.A. All rights reserved.
10 9 8 7 6 5 4 3 2 1

For my friends Crystal and Donny,
who know the secret about the goblins

I'm sorry," said Spence's mother
as she turned off Spence's favorite television show.
"No more television until you pick up your toys."

"I don't want to pick up my toys," said Spence,
frowning at his mother.

"No toys, no television," said his mother firmly.

Spence frowned even more.
He wished a mean old bear would come
and take his mother away.
Then he would never have to pick up his toys,
and he could watch television all the time.

He stomped angrily to his room.

He took a piece of paper and a crayon,
and he drew a big mean old bear.

Suddenly, the bear started to move.
He stretched his arms and wiggled his paws.
Then he walked right off the paper.

"Well," growled the bear, "here I am!"

"Are you a mean old bear?" asked Spence doubtfully.
"The meanest!" snarled the bear, scowling at Spence.

"Are you going to take my mother?" asked Spence.
"That's what I'm here for," grunted the bear.
He had grown ten times bigger
and now almost filled Spence's room.
He had enormous paws, the size of kitchen sinks,
and feet the size of bathtubs.

"Where are you going to take my mother?"
asked Spence meekly.

"To my cave in the dark woods," rumbled the bear,
showing Spence his long, sharp teeth.
"Are you going to bite my mother?" asked Spence.
"I might," rasped the bear.

Spence thought about how the bear was going to take
his mother to the dark woods
and into a cave.
His mother might be really scared.
What if the bear bit her?

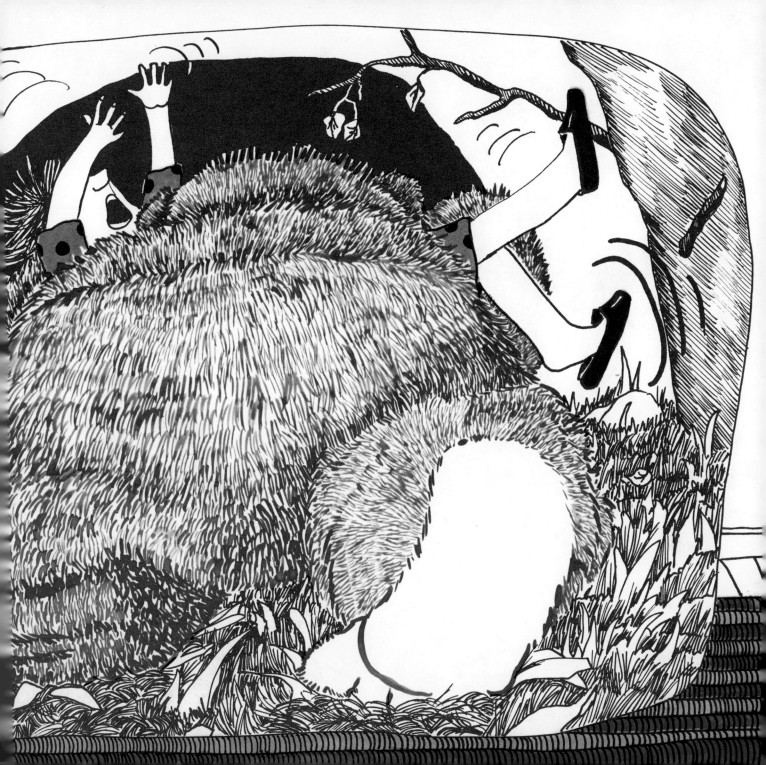

"Well," growled the bear impatiently,
"I haven't got all day."
And he opened Spence's door.

He had to duck low to squeeze himself through,
and his bathtub feet made loud thumping sounds
as he stomped down the hall.

Spence didn't know a mean old bear
was going to be *this* big.
Spence didn't want the bear to take his mother.
He wished he hadn't wished for a mean old bear.

Spence squeezed past the bear and ran to his mother.
He threw his arms around her and buried his face in her lap.

"Why, Spence, you're shaking all over,"
said his mother.
"There's a mean old bear," said Spence,
"and he's coming to get you."
"There is?" said Spence's mother, surprised.
"Don't worry. No mean old bear is going to get me.
I can get pretty mean, too,"
and she wiggled her fingers and growled.
She made Spence laugh.

Spence's mother gave him a big, long hug.
He took a little peek from under his arm.

The bear had grown much smaller,
and he didn't look mean at all
as he padded back to Spence's room.

Spence ran down the hall.
There was no bear in his room,

only the one Spence had drawn.
And he was only in crayon, on a piece of paper.
Spence crumpled the paper bear
and threw him in the wastepaper basket.

Then he went and picked up his toys.